Finding A Balance

Dieneria Brown

DEDICATION

To my mother: Thank you for always supporting my ambitions. From when I was younger and dreamed of being a princess to now when I desire to be a starving author. Your constant support and belief in me has helped me make it this far. I know I may not say it enough but I love you and appreciate all the sacrifices you have made to give me the best of everything.

To Mrs. Simchak: Thank you for developing my interest in writing, who knows where I would be without you. You gave me confidence in my writing in sixth grade, were the basis for my college essays, and the editor of this book. You have been there for my writing and I for a very long time and I appreciate all the time and effort you have put in.

CONTENTS

THE SEARCH

The graduation caps filled the air and the crowd let out a roaring cheer. Standing there on the grassy field amidst the cheerful chaos, I knew the worst three years of my life were over. Before I could take in the magnitude of this moment, I was enveloped in Mom's arms. There were tears streaming down my mother's face, and she was making muffled sounds into my shoulder. Over her shoulder I could see Dad mouthing, "She's been like this all day!" as he rolled his eyes. I tried, but failed, to suppress a chuckle. Mom looked up, pointing her mascara-stained face at me and asked, "What are you laughing at?"

"Oh it's nothing, Mom; I'm just laughing at Dad."

"You two are making funny of me again, aren't you? I'm sorry that I get a little sentimental when I see my little girl graduating," she said while sniffling.

"You're more than 'a little sentimental'; you're acting like she died! You might as well have put on all black and told people you were mourning," said Dad, which caused me to erupt in laughter. Mom didn't find it quite as funny.

Mom was even more upset when I refused to let her take me out to an expensive lunch. Instead we went to my favorite local diner. It was a little diner with neon lights and a red roof, which had a giant coffee cup protruding from it. We sat in a booth in the corner that had a miniature broken-down jukebox on the table. An older man with a receding hairline and three pens sticking out of his pocket took our order. He meandered through the diner in this slow methodical way. His feet never seemed to leave the ground; he just shuffled his black loafers across the black and white tiles.

"I'm surprised you like this restaurant. The service here is so slow," said my mother in a mocking tone.

"I know. I'm usually the one to complain about anything that takes longer than five minutes, but sometimes I want a slower-paced atmosphere. Besides, this place is so nice and homey."

"Well, I'm glad you picked this restaurant because a diner is probably all we can afford after sending you to college and law school," said Dad in a teasing tone.

"Harold, do not be such a Debbie downer. Our little girl is going to be a big time lawyer, making millions in no time."

"I see someone's trying to kiss up before you hit it big. But seriously, Jane, I am very proud of you, and I am certain that you will be successful and pay me back all that tuition money."

"Harold!"

"I'm just joking; have a sense of humor."

A few days later the tides had definitely changed. Unlike many of my classmates, I had not secured a job before graduation. Though I had done clinic hours at two different law firms and had "connections" with judges in my area, I was not offered a single job. So during the days following my graduation, when all my former classmates were either still celebrating or on their last vacation before starting at some law firm, I was filling out applications and booking interviews.

After a week of non-stop job hunting, it was time for my first interview. I stood in front of my mirror in my best two-piece suit. It skated over the curves of my body, leaving me with a boxy shape. The matte black suit stood out from the colors that exploded within my room. My eyes scanned the portion of my room that I could see in the mirror: my orange and white bedspread that had travelled with me from my undergraduate dorm room, the turquoise digital clock that was teetering on the edge of my nightstand the same way it used to when I was in high school, the laptop with a hot pink cover that I had gotten at the beginning of law school. Usually my room reminded me of various wonderful memories, but in that moment all I was reminded of was how long I had wanted to be a lawyer and how much of my life I would have wasted if that dream never came true. Taking one deep breath, I tried to push all the anxiety into the back of my mind and turn my focus once again to my reflection. My make-up was minimal, and my brunette hair was slicked into a bun that strategically hid my honey highlights. As I stared in the mirror, my reflection looked at least five years older, if not more, than the one I saw the previous day.

The train rocked methodically as it sped through the subway tunnels. My eyes were glued to the thick windowpane, watching as the tunnel walls and an occasional train flashed by. The flickering lights within the train only added to my stress-induced migraine. I pushed and squeezed out of the train, up the escalators, and to the street in a passive aggressive fashion. I used my brief case to maneuver people out of my way and whispered practically inaudible "excuse me's". Four blocks into my trek, I regretted my choice in footwear. In my rush that morning, I had assumed that my clunky grandma heels would be more comfortable than my stilettos, but I had forgotten that they were one size too small. The patent leather was eroding the skin on the top of my foot, and the point of the toe was ramming my toes against each other. My feet were literally pulsating as the receptionist told me,

"You're fifteen minutes early. Mr. Bradstock will be with you momentarily."

Sitting in the stark, almost sterile waiting area, I couldn't help but notice how young the receptionist was and frankly how unprofessional she looked. She wasn't dressed inappropriately or anything of that sort; she just wasn't dressed as professional as she could be. I felt bad judging, her but Mom's life lessons had apparently sunk in.

"Jane, listen, if you want to be a lawyer you're going to have to sacrifice a lot, and you cannot just be like everyone else; you must be better. Don't let the media fool you; this is still a man's world."

Before I could dwell anymore on how much I was turning into my mother, Mr. Bradstock came out of the meeting room adjacent to the waiting area. If I had any hope that this interview would go well, it evaporated as I saw the train of well-dressed male baby-boomers following him out of the meeting room. The secretary confirmed my suspicion that this was a partners' meeting. As I saw Mr. Bradstock coming over, I mustered all my strength in the hope of not looking defeated.

"You must be Ms..." said Mr. Bradstock as he simultaneously searched for my name on my résumé and shook my hand.

"Claremonte," I said gently with a smile.

"Ah, yes, Ms. Claremonte. Are you ready for your interview?"

"Yes, of course."

"Good. Follow me."

Mr. Bradstock continued with mundane talk as we walked towards the office. The conversation jumped from the weather, to the traffic, to the current news stories. As soon as we entered his office, the mood and conversation drastically changed. It felt like more of an interrogation than an interview.

"To be frank, I don't see why you applied for this position."

"Umm, what? I'm sorry I don't quite understand what you mean by that. I applied for this position because I would love to practice with your firm. Your firm is extremely well-known in this area for having the best lawyers in the field of patent law."

"But based on your transcript and résumé, it is clear that you have little or no experience in patent law."

"Although, my focus was not originally on patent law, I have realized that it is where my interests lie," I said, though I knew it wasn't one hundred percent true. I had taken interest in various law fields throughout law school and had never settled on one.

"Ms. Claremonte, based on your GPA, recommendations, and various cases you have worked on, I think you will make an exceptional lawyer. I am willing to give you a place in this firm, but you will need training in patent law. I am willing to offer you a paid internship so you can learn the ropes. Once you get the hang of it, which I'm sure won't take long, you can become a full-time lawyer here."

"Excuse me for being forward, but what would the salary be for an intern?"

"You would only work part-time, I don't know the exact numbers off the top of my head, but I would assume you would need another job to supplement your income. Until you were promoted, of course."

"Mr. Bradstock, I do not want to waste your time, so I will tell you right now that I cannot accept that position. In this economy I just can't afford to take a job that will not support me financially. But I do appreciate your offering me this opportunity."

All my interviews that week and the three weeks that followed ended in the same or similar ways. Either I was unqualified, too young, the salary was ridiculously low, or a combination of both. There was only one thing left to do; call my mother.

"Jane! I haven't heard from you in so long. How have you been? Is life as amazing as you imagined it would be after graduation? Harold, come here! Jane's on the line!"

"Oh, God," I muttered.

"What was that, dear?"

"Hmm. I didn't say anything."

"Oh, ok. Here's Dad."

"Hi Daddy. How's retirement treating you?"

"Good. Your mom's driving me crazy."

"Shut up, Harold," said Mom in a muffled voice from behind him.

"So how has the job search been? Have you proved me wrong yet?"

"Well, actually that's why I'm calling, I've been having a hard time finding work."

"This is exactly what I told you would happen. You and your mother guilt tripped me into paying for you to go to law school, and now I'm out of tens of thousands of dollars, and you still can't find work."

"Harold, stop yelling at her. She couldn't have predicted the future. Besides she just graduated. She still has plenty of time to get a job."

"I'm not yelling. I'm just stating that I was right, and you two were wrong. Ha!"

"Don't listen to him, Jane. He's just grumpy because I've been teasing him about that stupid car he brought.

"It's not stupid. It's a diamond in the rough!"

"Calm down, Harold. Now as I was saying, Jane, your father got sucked into buying some old piece of junk car because the dealer convinced him it was a good project for a retiree to work on."

"I didn't know Dad knew how to fix cars."

"That's the problem. He doesn't." she said, as she quietly snickered.

"Well, Dad seems to be right. I did make him waste tens of thousands of dollars."

"Jane, stop being so melodramatic. Just because it's not easy to get a job doesn't mean it's not possible."

"It seems pretty impossible to me. I have applied to every job that I am even remotely qualified for, and I can't seem to get one. Everyone keeps telling me how I should apply again when I'm older and have more experience, but how am I supposed to get experience if no one will hire me?"

"Qualifications are great and all, but that is not always the way to get a job. Sometimes the best way to get a job is to call in a favor."

"Whom would I call for a favor? I tried asking the judges I worked for, and none of them have open positions."

"Maybe they know someone who does. You just need to call around to people you know and ask if they know of any positions for you. You should also try going to networking events and passing out your business card."

"Networking events? That seems like a shot in the dark."

"I don't know, Jane. I'm just giving you suggestions. The most important thing is that you don't give up."

"Ok, Mom. I'll talk to you later."

"Bye, sweetie. Keep your chin up."

I'd gone to networking events while I was in law school, and they obviously had not worked for me, so that appeared out of the question. For the rest of the day I emailed my old professors, judges I worked for, and anyone in law whose business card I happened to have. Three days later I got a response from Sue, a girl who graduated from my law school two years prior to me. We hadn't really kept in touch over the last year, but before that we had been very good friends. The email was short and to the point:

"You can come for an interview tomorrow at one-thirty."

The waiting room of Sue's firm was identical to all the other waiting rooms I'd been in: sterile, stark, and silent. I was starting to wonder if Sue even knew who I was because her reply had been so blunt. I was expecting her to ask me how I'd been doing and send a greeting to my parents, but instead I got a one-sentence response. Before I could dwell on it for long, a man was introducing himself to me.

"Hello, I'm Matthew Jameston. I will be conducting your interview today."

"Oh, okay," I said, visibly startled. Where was Sue and why wasn't she giving me my interview?

The interview seemed to go well. Afterwards Matthew walked me out and said he would be in touch. When I got home, my curiosity got the best of me, and I called Sue on her cell. The call went straight to voicemail, and I left a short message asking her to call me back when she got a chance. A week passed, and I still had not gotten a call back from Sue, but I did get one from Mr. Jameston he said that there was a position for me and I could start work immediately. I was beyond excited and immediately called Mom to share the news. I thought Harold and she were going to give themselves heart attacks from all the screaming they were doing. I smoothly talked my way out of having a "Jane-got-a-job celebratory party" and made some excuse to get off the phone. I didn't tell my parents this, but the whole Sue situation was really bothering me. I just couldn't understand why she was avoiding me. I decided to put those concerns aside and relish in the happiness and security of having a job.

THE WEDDING

I was finally ready. All my bridesmaids left me so I could have a moment to myself. I stood looking at the bride in the mirror. My eyes were darting from my stark white ball gown, to my sparkling jewelry, to my brown ringlets floating under my veil. As I looked at myself in the mirror, all I could think about was the last time I was in a wedding dress. I was four years old, and it was the day of Mom's wedding. Four-year-old me sat in my room, fully adorned as a bride. The gown I was wearing, which was obviously too big for my toddler frame, belonged to my mother. I hated my soon-to-be stepfather; he was harsh and strict, nothing like my real father. In an attempt to get me excited for the wedding Mom got me all dolled up in her wedding attire. To her dismay, not even that had cheered me up.

For the entirety of my mother's wedding, I was in a solemn mood. My facial expressions and body language were more suited to a funeral than a wedding. At the time it seemed as if my life was over and that Mom was making the biggest mistake of her life. Luckily Mom's judgment was better than mine, and Harold turned out to be her soul mate and an amazing father to me. Though it took some time, I eventually considered Harold to be my father. My real father moved out of state after his divorce from my mother, and the only adult male who was left in my life was Harold.

Thinking about that day made me happy to know that Mom was here and approved of Rickford. I hoped my wedding remained drama free for the rest of the day. Just thinking about what could go wrong was making me anxious. I could hear my heart beating slowly, then faster and louder. It was rhythmic, almost soothing, and then music started; my heart fluttered. I dashed toward the door, as fast as one can dash in five-inch heels, and practically tackled my stepfather who was waiting outside.

"Careful. The last thing you want to do is break your ankle on your wedding day."

"I know, but we're late!"

"The music just started and the aisle is just two feet in front of us through that door. We are not late. Relax, catch your breath, and smile."

I intertwined my arm within his and took a deep breath. As the church doors opened I saw everyone's heads whip around and smiles on their faces. As we inched toward the aisle with my white train floating behind me, I could see Rickford's beaming face.

When we exchanged our vows, it felt like no one was in the room but us. Before I knew it, the ceremony was over, and Rickford was carrying me back down the aisle through all the smiling and crying people who were sending their congratulations and best wishes. When we got to the church's front steps, Rickford put me down and all the men withdrew to the side. The women pushed forward, in anticipation. I turned my back to the crowd and counted, "1...2...3", and with that I sent my bouquet flying over my head and landing amongst a pile of women's anxious arms. Two women, one a bridesmaid and one a beautiful woman I'd never seen before, eventually caught it.

"Do you think they're going to fight each other for it?" Rickford whispered into my ear with a smirk.

"Is there any other option?" I replied with a wink.

Sadly our sarcasm had no effect on the ladies, and instead of brawling they chose to split the bouquet into two.

"I told you we should have invited your crazy Great Aunt Blake. Civilized people are no fun," Rickford said jokingly as he gestured toward the women who had split the bouquet.

"Trust me; crazy is no fun, either" I said thinking back to all my memories of Aunt Blake.

On the way to the reception Rickford did not want to talk about anything except Aunt Blake, not even about the wedding. I finally gave in and agreed to tell him an Aunt Blake story.

"Alright I'll tell you one; just stop begging"

"Okay, I'm listening."

"You get to pick: Thanksgiving or Easter?"

"Does the Easter story involve a bunny suit?"

"What? No. I said she was crazy not hilarious. In the Easter story Aunt Blake lost my little cousin Amy. In the Thanksgiving story she brought a criminal to our Thanksgiving dinner."

"The criminal one sounds interesting. Tell that one."

"Okay, but this story doesn't involve an animal suit either."

"I guess I'll I have to live with that disappointment" said Rickford with a smile, "Now stop stalling and tell the story; we're only fifteen minutes away from the reception."

"Calm down! I'm not stalling! I was fifteen or sixteen years old, and we were having Thanksgiving at my parents' house in Idaho. There was a little bit of snow on the ground, but the storm had stopped and all our family had arrived, except crazy Aunt Blake. My mother, who adores Aunt Blake, was frantic. She kept saying things like 'Where could she be?,' 'What if she got into a terrible accident?,' and 'I'm calling the police! She could be dead.' Luckily no one let her call the police because fifteen minutes later, in walked Aunt Blake along with a guest. Her guest was a man with a scruffy beard and dingy hair, wearing overalls with no shirt underneath, he was missing his two front teeth."

"What?"

"Shhh! Let me tell the story."

"Okay. Okay."

"So, as I was saying Aunt Blake walked in with this man who was filthy and whom no one had ever seen before. Uncle Bard asked her, 'Is that your new boyfriend, Blake?' The entire room erupted into laughter and my mother's eyes darted from person to person, giving them dirty looks.

'Oh, you mean Max? Nah he's just some guy I meet during my layover.'

'I'm glad you met a friend, Blake, and he is welcome to stay for dinner,' said my mother with a genuine smile. There were gasps and murmurs throughout the room, but no one had the courage to challenge her.

We all gathered around the table for Thanksgiving dinner with Max sitting in between my mother and Aunt Blake. As the dinner progressed, my mother kept glancing at Max and furrowing her brow. It had been over an hour since Max arrived, and he hadn't said a word to anyone, not even Aunt Blake.

'Max, why don't you tell us how you met Blake?' said my mother, who was obviously hoping to get Max to open up.

Max's eyes got big, and he kept looking from Blake to mother. The entire table was awkwardly silent. Blake seemed unaware of the silence and continued to shovel food down her throat.

'Blake, dear, I'm afraid I may have startled your guest.'

'Max is easily startled. I think he is afraid your going to kick him out if he tells you how we met.'

'I would never do such a thing. I told you, Max, you are welcome in my home, and that is what I meant. There is nothing you could say to make me change my mind but I am sorry if my curiosity and prying has made you uncomfortable.'

'Go on Max. Tell her how we met.'

'I was begging for money outside the airport, and I asked her for some money. That's how we met'

'Oh, your not doing the story justice. Let me tell it. So I was going outside the terminal during my layover to have a smoke. There was Max with this sign, you know the ones on pieces of cardboard, asking for donations. So I went up to him and asked him how much he needed. He said he just needed enough to get some food and a hotel room because he just got released from jail. Instead of just giving him money, I decided to get him a ticket and bring him with me so that he could have a real Thanksgiving.'"

"That was very nice of her."

"Nice? Yes, but also very stupid. She didn't ask this man anything about himself. We were all just lucky that he wasn't a murder or kidnapper. That's the problem with Aunt Blake she is always so busy being nice that she doesn't think her plans through. Which is exactly why I did not invite her to our wedding."

"What could she have possibly done at our wedding?"

"I don't know. You never know what someone like her is going to do. She is just so spontaneous."

"If you can't even think of one thing she would have done wrong, then there was no reason not to invite her to our wedding. You probably really hurt her feelings by not inviting her."

"I realize that I may have hurt her feelings, but I had to do what I thought was best. Aunt Blake would do something such as give our wedding cake away to a homeless man because he looked hungry. Though she obviously never means any harm, she often ends up causing problems for the ones she loves the most. I just did not want to have to worry about her doing something ridiculous on my wedding day."

"I understand your concern, but a wedding is about sharing your love and happiness with your family and friends. I think you got too caught up in making everything perfect and forgot about the point of all this. I still think you owe her an apology, but right now we need to go to our reception." Rickford seemed ready to put this conversation behind us and have a good time, but I was still feeling guilty.

As we were walking up to the doors of the ballroom we could hear the laughter and chatter of our guests wafting out. Rickford lead the way, with my arm linked to his, into the ballroom. Everything from the chandeliers to the napkin holders were gold and white and emblazoned with our initials. It was better than I had imagined it would be.

"Why are you staring at the ceiling like tourists in New York stare at skyscrapers? Is this not the way you planned for the reception to look?" asked Rickford.

"I'm just taking it all in. It looks even better now that I see it in person and not just in sketches or parts here and there."

"I'm glad you like it, especially since, you spent months planning," he sarcastically responded.

"If I had not spent months planning it, we would not have had a wedding. You weren't going to plan it. You barely even gave suggestions when I was planning it."

"That's because you care more about the wedding than I do. I wanted to marry you, not have this elaborate ceremony, but I knew that you always dreamed of having a fairytale wedding. Which is why I let you take the reins on the decorating and planning."

"How romantic of you!" I said, mimicking his infamous sarcastic tone. "Of course, it had nothing to do with your being lazy."

"I am not lazy. I am just selective in what I use my energy for," said Rickford with a smirk.

"I see. So is that why you managed to muster up enough strength to go to all the cake and entrée tastings?"

"Exactly. Those are the types of things that are really important when it comes to weddings," he said as he led me to our seats.

The dinner was going well, and everyone was having a good time. Rickford and Mom were bonding over how much they wished Aunt Blake were here, while Uncle Bard and I rolled our eyes. The toasts were fairly ordinary; everyone was saying how perfect we were together and wishing us a long happy marriage, but then it was Dad's turn. Though Dad was infamous for embarrassing me, I was not worried this time because Mom told me earlier that she had proofread his speech. I knew there was no way that she would let him say anything even mildly embarrassing. It started off with his talking about how much I had grown up and led into a story about me as child:

"Jane has always been a kind person and a people pleaser. I remember one particular instance when she was five years old. It was the Fourth of July, and everyone was out back having a barbeque. Jane's mother wanted her to wear this white dress, but her grandmother wanted her to wear a red dress. The two of them had been arguing back in forth about it for a few minutes, so they told Jane she could just decide for herself which dress to wear. Poor little Jane didn't want to hurt either of their feelings by picking the other dress, so she came outside in nothing but her underwear. Though Jane now wears clothes in public, she hasn't changed much from her five-year-old self. When it comes down to it, Jane will still do anything to please others. So, you Rickford are a very lucky man to have such a selfless woman as your wife. And no worries, everyone. I made sure to include the picture of Jane on the Fourth of July in the slideshow!"

"I can't wait for the slideshow," Rickford said enthusiastically to the table.

"Harold, that is not the toast I approved," said Mom with a stern look.

"I knew you would never let me tell that story, so I showed you a different speech. Wedding toasts are supposed to have embarrassing stories in them. Besides, I could have told much more embarrassing stories, but I thought I'd let the pictures speak for themselves."

"You let Dad pick the pictures for the slideshow?" I frantically asked Mom.

"I didn't know what this whole slideshow thing was. We didn't have slideshows at weddings when I was younger. Harold said he knew what it was, so I let him do it."

The slideshow was more embarrassing than I could have possibly imagined. Dad managed to find pictures of me at my worst moments. Such as, when I got my wisdom teeth pulled and had chipmunk cheeks, and the time I tried to dye my own hair and it turned a bright orange. As if having these horrendous moments viewed by all my family and friends wasn't embarrassing enough, all my pictures were juxtaposed with the adorable pictures of Rickford, which his mother had picked out. After the montage of my embarrassing moments was over, it was time for the dancing.

"Come on, chipmunk," said Rickford referencing the post-wisdom teeth removal picture. "It's time for the first dance."

The emcee announced the first dance and then proceeded to play our song. Towards the end of our dance, Dad cut in. For the entire father-daughter dance I could hear him muttering "1..2...3...1...2...3" repeatedly, while staring at his shoes. I guess this was a trick he had learned in the ballroom dancing classes Mom forced him to go to prior to the wedding.

"Harold, look at this," said Mom when Dad went back to their table.

"That's wonderful! You got the whole father-daughter dance on tape!"

"It would be wonderful if you weren't staring at your feet and muttering like a crazy person the entire dance."

"Its your fault for sending me to those stupid classes. I danced just fine before."

"No, you didn't. You danced off beat and looked ridiculous. You still look ridiculous now, but at least you're on beat!"

"He couldn't have been that bad a dancer. You two used to go out dancing all the time, and you always would talk about how much fun it was," I interjected.

"I was just blinded by love back then, and I obviously still am, since I still let him wear these ridiculous bowties," said Mom as she gently tugged at Dad's shiny gold bowtie.

"You love my bowties and my dancing! That's it! I'm going to show you how good a dancer I am," said Dad as he pulled Mom to the dance floor. When they came back from the dance floor, Mom and Rickford pulled me to the side.

"Jane, I don't want you to get upset. This was my idea, so don't blame Rickford," said Mom with a worried look.

"We just thought you would regret it if she wasn't here. She is family, and I know you would never want to hurt her feelings," said Rickford with a forced smile. Before I could say anything, Aunt Blake walked up to us.

"This is just absolutely beautiful, Jane. Did you plan it all yourself?"

"Yes, I did. Can I talk to you, in private?"

"Of course," said Aunt Blake as I led her to an isolated table in the corner of the room.

"I'm not exactly sure what Rickford and Mom told you but..."

"They didn't really tell me anything. I just got a call asking if I could make it to the reception on such short notice. I told them I wasn't invited, but they said you wanted me here. So, I threw on a dress and caught a cab."

"They were right; I do want you here. Originally I hadn't invited you because I remembered your homeless Thanksgiving guest and the Easter fiasco. I know you never mean, to but sometimes you're so focused on helping people that you do things that end up causing problems. After talking to Rickford, I realized how much I wanted you here because, even though you occasionally do something out of the ordinary, your family and I can't remember a family event where you weren't with us. I hope you can accept my apology and enjoy the rest of your night."

"Of course I can accept your apology. I know I'm an eccentric and spontaneous person and that can be hard to deal with sometimes. My mother always told me that even though my plans did not always work out perfectly, the important part was that I had good intentions. I know that sometimes when I'm trying to do good, it ends up back-firing, but everyone makes silly mistakes. As long as I am trying my hardest to do what is right, I'm proud of myself."

"I guess I never thought of it that way but you're right. No one can predict the future so the most you can do is have good intentions and hope for the best outcome."

The rest of the night was fantastic. With the entire family in attendance, the dancing continued until late into the night, and everyone was having a good time. I even saw Aunt Blake and Uncle Bard laughing together at one point. Though I wished Rickford and Mom had not been so secretive about inviting Aunt Blake I was glad she was with us. The wedding just didn't mean as much without all my friends and family there to enjoy it with me.

The next morning Rickford and I left for our weeklong honeymoon in the Caribbean. We spent the week having our own little adventure, and we both managed to put work aside, which was rare for us since we were both lawyers and seemed to have an endless amount of work.

THE OFFICE

As I watched the Starbucks barista preparing my drink, I could practically hear the ticking of a clock. My office was only five buildings down, but I needed to be through the door, down the corridor, and in the elevator in the next three minutes. I had to beat Steven to the office.

As the elevator doors opened on the seventh floor, I let out a sigh of relief. The place looked empty. While I was walking to my small corner office, a large hand firmly grasped my shoulder.

"Good Morning, Mrs. Braxton," said Steven with a cheery smile.

"Oh. Good Morning St... uh Mr. Jackson. I didn't realize anyone was in the office."

"Sorry. I didn't mean to startle you. I've been here since six," said Steven, still obnoxiously cheery for so early in the morning.

As soon as I walked into my office, I checked my clock. It was seven forty-five. Partners didn't need to be here until eight. Steven must have known something I didn't. Why else would he have been here so early?

At nine a.m. sharp the firm meeting began. The head of the firm, Sue Rockwill, was one of the most successful female lawyers on the East Coast. She demanded perfection and ridiculed anything less.

She stood at the front of the boardroom next to the projector, her bluish-green eyes darting from the screen to her audience as she presented.

"What is that noise!" said the surprisingly deep and booming voice of Ms. Rockwill. All eyes turned to the new intern who was attempting to text under the boardroom table. "Poor guy," I thought. "He doesn't know Ms. Rockwill has hearing like a wolf and teeth just as sharp."

"I realize that in your high school, your teachers may not have been able to hear the incessant clicking of your Blackberry, but I can. And I cannot imagine who you could be texting that is worth being fired for. This is a law firm, not some eighteen-and-under club. Put your phone away and get a suit jacket to go over that shirt. And while you're at it, you might want to shave because no one is impressed with that fuzz you call a beard."

"Aunt Viv, I'm twenty-one, not eighteen," said the intern. Murmuring filled the room and Ms. Rockwill's face turned a bright red.

"Everyone but Tim, out!"

The whole firm scurried to their desks and worked on anything they could find; if they couldn't find anything, they pretended to work. Aside from the sound of furious typing, the floor was silent. Though every once in a while you would hear a high-pitched scream or expletive wafting from the boardroom. Thirty minutes later Ms. Rockwill's nephew sulked out of the room. Before I could quench my curiosity, I heard Ms. Rockwill commanding me to the boardroom.

"Sue," I said, "you didn't have to be that hard on the kid. You know he looks up to you. Not to mention he's family."

"You're right; we are family, and that is exactly why I had to be hard on him. Let's be honest, Jane; this is still a man's world. You know better than anyone that I don't want to hurt Tim's feelings, but I had no choice. I can't have people thinking I'm soft or that I have some sort of maternal instinct. No one would take me seriously. Lawyers are supposed to be sharks not mama bears."

"Don't you think sometimes you can be a little overly cautious?"

"No, I do not. When it comes to my job, there is no such thing as being too cautious."

"Oh, really? How about when you refused to acknowledge my interview or talk to me for a month when I first worked here?"

"I had to create separation between us, Jane. I didn't want people thinking that I gave you the job because we were school friends."

"You wouldn't speak to me for an entire month! You didn't even tell me why we weren't speaking."

"I was just doing what was in the best interest of both of our jobs. I couldn't have people thinking that I was using my power in this firm to give my friends free handouts. You had to prove yourself without any association to me."

"I know now why you did it, but I still think a month-long silent treatment was extreme. Even now you won't let people see us talking together unless it is strictly about work."

"That is called keeping your professional and private relationships separate. It is appropriate office etiquette."

"We are friends, not secret lovers!"

"Look, Jane, I may go above and beyond sometimes when it comes to remaining appropriately professional at work, but I have learned that that is necessary to maintain emotional distance. As a woman in a historically male profession, I am scrutinized harder than my male associates, and I refuse to give anyone any reason to doubt my professionalism or my skills."

I nodded, remembering how hard I had to work just to find a job after college. I had to come begging to Sue for a job because I was getting barely any offers, even though I had graduated *cum laude* in my class. But Steven had offers from every firm he applied to and was "just negotiating the numbers," when making his decision, even though he had only been in the middle of our class.

"I know what a man's world the legal profession is. Don't think I've forgotten the whole Steven incident," I said.

"Let's be honest. The reason you don't like Steven is that he is 'too happy' all the time."

"Only psychotic people are that happy. He's a lawyer, for God's sake. What could be that joyous in his life?" I responded. Sue's boisterous laugh filled the room.

"Besides, most of the time he's not just happy. He's snide and egotistical," I continued.

"Alright. Enough about Steven. Let's just go to lunch so you can tell me this big news," said Sue, visibly annoyed.

"It's not that big of a deal," I said, hoping that Sue would feel the same way.

As we sat at our favorite restaurant, I tried to keep the subject on our most recent corporate corruption case. We talked about various strategies for keeping our obviously guilty client out of jail, even though he had smuggled millions of dollars from his company. But Sue was a lawyer, and my constant fidgeting and lack of eye contact were dead giveaways that I was anxious. She knew something was going on, and she seemed angry that I wasn't telling her.

"I highly doubt your big news had anything to do with this case. So let's stop avoiding the subject. Whatever it is, you need to tell me because the longer you wait, the angrier I am going to get," said Sue.

"Well... it's good news actually. You see I am kind of pregnant"

"What! Pregnant! What do you mean 'kind of'? Kind of like you kind of could not be pregnant?"

"No, I am definitely pregnant."

"How is this good news? You can no longer work."

"What are you talking about? Of course I can work. I'm pregnant not incompetent. What is the worse thing that could happen?"

"What if your water breaks in the middle of the courtroom? And the ambulance doesn't come in time, and I have to deliver your baby!" said Sue.

"Well, since this isn't some trashy Lifetime movie, I don't think we have to worry about that happening."

"Obviously, that was an extreme circumstance, but honestly, Jane, this is a huge liability. What if you have pretend labor..."

"You mean false labor?"

"Yeah, that thing. And you don't come to work and miss a big court date, and it turns out to be a false alarm. Or even worse, what if I do make you partner and then you want to take maternity leave and end up not coming back. Then what am I going to do?"

"I'm barely in my first trimester. Maternity leave is a long time away."

"How long exactly?"

"Well, assuming everything goes well, sometime in the late third trimester, so about seven months from now."

"Seven months? This corporate corruption case won't even be over by then. Why didn't you tell me this sooner? I would never have put you on such a big case if I knew you were going to be popping out children and abandoning your work."

"First of all, I'm not octo-mom. I am having one child, not 'popping out children.' Second of all, I am not abandoning my work. I am going to be working until the day I go into labor, and I am going to come back as soon as I can."

"So, you're telling me your going to give birth and then immediately come back to work and leave your baby with some nanny? Because I find that very hard to believe. Mothers always want to stay with their babies and witness the first moments and crap."

"Just because I am going back to work doesn't mean I am going to miss the first moments. I am going to work not halfway across the world. Plenty of women balance being a mother and being a business woman, too."

"If you're just going to have some nanny raise your kid for you, I don't see why you're having it to begin with."

"This was not a planned pregnancy. I got pregnant and am married to the love of my life. What do you suggest I do?" I said beginning to get irritated with her attitude.

"Well, I think you're a little too far along for what I would suggest."

THE ARGUEMENT

"So, how did it go?" asked Rickford before I could even get my coat off.

"Horrible."

"It could not have gone that bad. I'm sure Sue was happy for you."

"If happy is the same thing as implying I should get an abortion. You're right. She was ecstatic!"

"What? She did not say that. She can't say that. A boss cannot tell an employee to get an abortion."

"Obviously she was not that explicit, Rickford. But she made it quite clear that was what she wanted me to do."

"Well, then I guess you have to quit."

"Have you lost your mind?"

"Jane, please calm down. I know your hormonal and all because of the baby, but there is no reason to scream."

"No reason to scream! You just told me to quit my job after I have spent my entire life working to get here and I am this close to making partner. All because I didn't like some comment my boss made?"

"It wasn't just some comment. She told you that you shouldn't have our baby. Don't you think that's a little extreme?"

"Of course she was out of line, but that's how Sue is. She speaks her mind and does not care whether it's p.c. or not."

"Exactly, and she doesn't care whether her decisions are controversial or not, either. Do you really think she is going to make you partner? You're pregnant, and she obviously is not happy with it. She is going to give the position to Steven just because he isn't pregnant."

"So, you think I should just give up without even trying?"

"Yes, I do. You shouldn't be working while you're pregnant anyways. It's not healthy for the baby."

"Is 'not healthy for the baby' code for I'm a sexist and think all women belong in the house? Because I don't see how my doing paperwork and appearing in court is going to hurt the baby."

"If I thought that, I wouldn't have married you. I know you are a business woman, and I respect that, but I don't think you should be doing that much walking around on your feet."

"How is it any more work than I do here? I don't see you cooking dinner or cleaning the house or getting groceries. And I'm pretty sure it's impossible to do those things while I'm sitting down."

"If you want me to do the house work, I will."

"No. I want you to support me in my career choices."

"Okay. I support you go fight for the partnership, but I don't think Sue's going to give it to you. All you're going to end up doing is stressing yourself out, which is harmful to the baby."

Sadly, this was not the last argument of this type. As my pregnancy advanced Rickford, got more and more paranoid. This paranoia led to him to worry constantly about my getting too stressed at work. It got to a point where it was impossible for me to talk to him about my day at the office. Anytime I mentioned my job or the case I was working on, he would say the same thing: 'You're too stressed. Why don't you just take a break? The firm has to give you maternity leave."

No matter how many times I tried to explain to Rickford that I was not anymore stressed than usual or that I did not want to take maternity leave, he just didn't understand. The baby seemed to be pushing us apart instead of bringing us together.

Since I obviously couldn't get through to Rickford on my own, I decided to get someone to help me.

As we drove down the road toward the office building, we were silent. Rickford's hands gripped the steering wheel tightly, and his eyes were glued to the road. He had a classical music station playing in the background, which only seemed to add to the tension. He turned smoothly into the parking lot and parked in the spot adjacent to Dr. Lock's awning.

"Here we are," Rickford said, as he turned off the ignition.

"Ready to go in?" I asked, since he had made no effort to get out of the car. Rickford sat there with his seatbelt still on and stared at the awning.

"Do you really think we need this?"

"I thought you were okay with this."

"Well, I wasn't. I just didn't want to upset you. We don't need couple's therapy. Anything we need to talk about we can do without a stranger."

"We've been trying to talk about it on our own, and it hasn't been working. I just think an outsider may be able to help each of us see the other's perspective."

"I think we both see each other's perspective. You think that is fine for you to continue working, and I think that it is too stressful for you and the baby and that you need to take maternity leave. The problem is not that we do not understand each other's point of view. The problem is that we do not agree. A couple's therapist is not going to make either of us change our minds. We are both too stubborn for that."

"So, what do you suggest we do? Everyday I feel this animosity from you."

"It's not animosity you're feeling. It's worry. I'm worried about you, Jane. You're doing way too much. Your job is stressful and overwhelming. You could handle that before you were pregnant, but I think it is too much pressure for you now."

"How do you know that working and being pregnant is too much pressure for me? Shouldn't I be the judge of what I can handle?"

"In a perfect world, yes. But I know you. You are not going to admit that you're overwhelmed or that you need a break because you are too worried about making partner. Your own parents are pressuring you to make partner."

"My parents are not pressuring me, they are supporting me! Unlike you, they appreciate how hard I've worked and want to see me rewarded for that work."

"Calling you everyday asking you when you are going to know who made partner is not support. You can't sit here and tell me that having your parents getting their hopes up about your making partner is not stressful. They have such high expectations for you, and you are afraid of letting them down, so you do everything you can to please them. Even if that means taking on more responsibilities than you can handle."

"I can handle working and being pregnant. Plenty of women go to work while pregnant. It is not a big deal."

"Are those women competing to make partner at a top law firm under immense pressure? I don't know about other women, but I know that you cannot handle the pressure you're under. You are not getting enough sleep, and even though you deny it you are stressed. All this excess stress and lack of sleep is not healthy for you or the baby."

"This conversation is going nowhere. We are never going to agree on what is best for me."

"Exactly, and a couple's therapist is not going to help us agree."

"Fine. We can leave if that's what you want."

"I'm not driving us home until we reach a compromise."

"What type of compromise?"

"What if you just work part time?"

"If I start taking time off now, Sue is going to worry that I will not be reliable and I will never make partner."

"You could always make partner later in your career. This won't be your last opportunity to make partner."

"I don't understand why I have to put my career on hold and you don't. Making partner is important to me, and I am not going to sabotage my chances by taking time off right now."

"So much for a compromise," said Rickford as he started the car and pulled out of the parking spot.

After that conversation, Rickford stopped trying to convince me to quit working, but he continued to make comments about my putting too much stress on myself. In order to help pacify him, I decided to bring Rickford with me to my next couple of doctor's appointments. I thought hearing that the baby was healthy from an expert would help calm his nerves.

"Jane, I don't mean to rush you, but when exactly do you think your husband will get here?" asked Dr. Samson with that stereotypical doctor smile on his face.

"I'm not sure. My phone calls have been going straight to voicemail, but I'm sure he'll be here soon because he knows I'm waiting for him."

"Okay, dear. Well, since I have other patients waiting, I am going to go ahead and get them set up to give your husband time to get here. Is that okay with you?"

"Yes, that's fine. I'm sorry for the wait. I'm sure he'll be here any minute."

"No problem. I'll be back in few minutes," said Dr. Samson as he left the room and gently closed the door, leaving me alone and embarrassed.

I pulled my phone out of my purse and hit re-dial for the fifth time that day. Once again my phone went to voicemail.

"Rickford, it's Jane. This is the fifth time I've called you. I'm starting to get worried. Where are you? You told me you would meet me at the doctor's office forty-five minutes ago. Call me when you get this message."

Since, calling Rickford was obviously not getting me anywhere, I decided to call his secretary.

"Good Afternoon. You've reached the Lamb and King Firm. This is Stacey. How may I help you?"

"Good Afternoon, Stacey. This is Jane, Rickford's wife. I was wondering if you knew when Rickford left the office because he was suppose to meet me almost an hour ago. He still hasn't arrived, and his cell phone is off."

"He must have forgotten, Jane, because he is still here meeting with a client. Would you like me to go get him?"

"No, that's fine."

"Okay. Well, I'll be sure to tell him you called."

"Thanks, Stacey. Have a nice day."

"Bye, you have a nice day also."

A few minutes later Dr. Samson popped his head in.

"Dr. Samson! My husband seems to have gotten caught up at work. So, let's just go on with the appointment without him."

"Alright. Let's start with an ultrasound. Let me just get my nurse to help me."

Later that evening when I was fixing dinner, I heard someone coming through the door.

"Jane, I'm home."

"I'm in the kitchen."

I could hear him putting his jacket in the closet and walking down the hall to his office to put his briefcase down.

"So, what are we having for dinner?" he asked as he walked into the kitchen.

"Lasagna. Let's go to the living room. We need to talk."

Rickford nonchalantly lead the way to the living room. I gently set myself down on the glossy leather coach next to the bookcase full of law books. Rickford sat down in the armchair to my right. The lamp cast a yellowish light on the gray hairs starting to emerge from his dark curls.

"So, what is it you wanted to talk about?"

"You were suppose to meet me at the doctor's office today. I left you multiple messages and you never called me back."

"Stacey told me she talked to you, so I saw no reason to call you and repeat what she already told you."

"Why didn't you call me to tell me you weren't coming to begin with?"

"I didn't have time. I was with a client. I assumed you would just continue with the appointment without me. Did the doctor say something was wrong with the baby?"

"No. The baby is fine"

"Then why are you angry?"

"Because it's okay for you to put work before the baby. But when I do the same thing, I'm being a horrible person?"

"Is that what this is about? You're angry because you think I was being hypocritical."

"Yes, I am angry that you think it's okay for you to put work before everything else, but when I just try to have a healthy balance of both, you lay a guilt trip on me. I'm also angry that you left me waiting at the doctor's office and embarrassed me."

"How did I embarrass you?"

"Dr. Samson and I were waiting for you for forty-five minutes! It was embarrassing being the pregnant woman whose husband stood her up at a prenatal doctor's appointment."

"I had to meet with my client. I honestly didn't think that you would wait for me. I thought you would have the appointment without me, and I planned on calling and telling you why I didn't make it after my meeting was over."

That night and the next couple of nights Rickford and I slept in different rooms. The fact that he was being so hypocritical upset me. He was making it seem as if his job was some how more important than mine. No matter how much I compared his missing the doctor's appointment for work to my working toward partner while pregnant, he did not see the similarities. In his mind it was not the same because I was 'putting the baby in danger by being stressed,' whereas he was just prioritizing. Apparently being pregnant meant that my only priority could be the baby.

THE DELIVERY

"Rickford! Rickford! Wake up!" I screamed as I shook him repeatedly.

"What? What is it? Are you going into labor?"

"Yes! Now hurry up and get up. I told you we should have packed an emergency bag."

"But the baby's not due for another two months, and its three o' clock in the morning!"

"Apparently, the baby doesn't care what time it is," I said, as I threw the first shirt and pants I could find onto my body.

"Okay. What should I do? Should I call an ambulance? Your not going to give birth here are you?" asked Rickford. His eyes bulged out of his head.

"Calm down. All your fidgeting and screaming is making me nervous. You get dressed and start packing a bag to take to the hospital. I'll call a cab."

Fifteen minutes and many contractions later, Rickford was helping me slide into the backseat of a cab.

"Oh, wow! You must be pretty far along!" said the taxi driver with a toothy smile.

"Very far along. We actually would like you to take us to the hospital," I said, while still keeping track of the time between the contractions.

"Of course, of course. Don't worry I'll get you there in no time. I wouldn't want you giving birth in the back of my cab," the driver said with a wink.

"Don't even joke about something like that," Rickford mumbled from the front seat. He was getting visibly paler by the minute, I noted.

"Are you sure you want to be in the room for the birth? Because you look like you're about to pass out now, and we haven't even gotten to the hospital yet."

"Of course I want to see our first child born. I'm just worried about our making it to the hospital in time. But you don't worry. Everything is taken care of. Just sit back and breath," said Rickford with a forced smile. He might have said it was worry, but I could see the fear in his eyes.

Rickford had called the hospital during the taxi ride to make sure my doctor was there and to have a wheelchair meet us outside the hospital. At the time I thought he was being absurd, but by the time we pulled up to the maternity wing, my contractions were so strong and close together that I could barely get out of the car, even with Rickford and the taxi driver's help. A nurse quickly wheeled the wheelchair right up to the car and helped the men lift me into the seat. As the nurse wheeled me into the hospital, the taxi driver told Rickford to just stay by my side and that he would bring the bags in. With a grateful smile, Rickford handed him a tip and dashed after me.

Throughout the entire labor process, Rickford was by my side, holding my hand, and talking me through the pain; this was the closest we had been in months.

"It's a girl!" said the red-headed nurse in her animated voice. I smiled as she handed me the little bundle of cloth. I saw little wisps of brown hair, and then her tiny pink hands. Finally I saw those piercing green eyes, and my heart was hers. But that joy quickly dissipated when Clara was snatched from my arms. "I'm sorry, Mrs. Braxton, but she needs to be in the Neonatal Intensive Care Unit. But you and your husband can come visit her in a little bit."

"Why does she have to go there? She screamed when she was born, so her lungs are working."

"Yes, they are, and that is wonderful. But she is almost two full months premature. Clara is not fully developed, and she needs to be watched constantly. Not to mention that her immune system is extremely weak, and we need to make sure she is in a sterile place where she is less likely to get sick. You should just get some rest. I will take good care of her; don't worry." And just like that, Clara was gone. As soon as the nurse left, the cold sterile room filled with a silent tension. Rickford hadn't talked to me ever since the doctor had told him that the baby's premature delivery was most likely caused by stress. I knew he blamed me and was completely convinced that it was selfish of me to go to work while carrying Clara. But I honestly did not think I was risking our baby's health. The doctor kept telling me everything was fine. How was I supposed to know that Clara was going to be premature? But in Rickford's mind, it didn't matter whether I knew or not. The problem was that I had taken that chance. And honestly, I was starting to agree with him. The fact that I made partner over Steven was not comforting me as I lay there, praying that Clara would be fine. In fact, if anything, it made me feel worse. How could I have ever thought a title on a plaque outside a partner's office was worth risking my daughter's life?

"Mr. and Mrs. Braxton, we need you down in the NICU immediately. Clara's left lung has collapsed, and we are going to need you to make medical decisions on her behalf."

Without a word Rickford jolted out of his seat toward the hall door, leaving me shocked and abandoned. A nurse quickly helped me into a wheelchair, and its rubber wheels hummed on the linoleum tile as she hurried me to the NICU. I watched

Rickford's sprinting form disappear around a corner, and I whispered prayers for Clara.

ABOUT THE AUTHOR

A graduating senior from the National Cathedral School for Girls, Dieneria Brown has always had a passion for writing. In this novella she interweaves her leadership roles in diversity and equality with her passion for writing to create a social commentary on the modern role of women.